Habari Gani? What's the News?

A KWANZAA STORY

by SUNDAIRA MORNINGHOUSE
PAINTINGS by JODY KIM

OPEN HAND PUBLISHING, LLC
P.O. Box 20207, Greensboro, NC 27420
336-292-8585/ fax 336-292-8588

OPEN HAND PUBLISHING, LLC

P.O. Box 20207, Greensboro, NC 27420
336-292-8585/ fax 336-292-8588

Book and cover design:
Deb Figen, Art & Design Services
Seattle, Washington

Library of Congress Cataloging-in-Publication Data

Morninghouse, Sundaira.
    Habari gani? = What's the news? / by Sundaira Morninghouse:
illustrations by Jody Kim. - - 1st ed.
        p.   cm.
    Summary : A family celebrates each day of Kwanzaa.
    ISBN 0-940880-39-3 : $14.95
    [1. Kwanzaa - - Fiction. 2. Afro-Americans - - Fiction.] I. Kim,
Jody, ill. II. Title.   III. Title: What's the news?
PZ7.M82693Hab 1992
[E] - - dc20
                                            92-12272
                                                CIP
                                                AC

_____
Printed in the United States of America
96   95   94   93   8 7 6 5 4 3 2

KWANZAA is the only nationally celebrated, indigenous, non-heroic African-American holiday in the United States. For many African-American families, December 26 through January 1 is a time of political and cultural expression and a "rededication to greater achievement and fuller, more meaningful lives." * Kwanzaa recognizes the African roots of African-Americans and, at the same time, reflects on and honors the history of African-Americans.

* **M. Karenga**

To everyone in my family —

my ancestors, my present-day relatives

and those yet to be born.

And to Dr. Maulana Karenga for his gift.

S. M.

For Ailea, Aja, Noah, Kahlil

and all the rare and colorful blooms.

For sundappled shadows on moist dark earth

fuchsia mango turquoise and plum

For all the seeds we consciously sow,

And especially the ones that we don't.

J. K.

Disemba 24 • December 24

"This year we're celebrating Kwanzaa," says Mama with an I-know-something-good smile.

I already know about Kwanzaa but Chaka doesn't so he keeps asking, "What Kanzaa, Mommy, what Kanzaa?"

"A real special time for all of us, baby, just you wait and see. But first, let's clear off the coffee table so we can prepare a place to celebrate."

Everybody gets busy. Baba, Mama, Chaka and me. Baba brings a big box into the living room and puts it on the floor beside the coffee table. Chaka and Mama take our everyday things to the closet while I dust the table and spread our *kente* cloth across it. Soon we are ready.

"To help us prepare our table I've made up a few verses to say along with each object we'll place here."

"Am I gonna get a turn, Mama?"

"Chaka, everybody has a turn at Kwanzaa," says Baba, "even me."

Then Mama begins, "*Mkeka* mat, *mkeka* mat. Please hand me the *mkeka* mat."

I give Mama the *mkeka* mat because I know it's the straw mat from our kitchen table.

"Thank you, Kia," says Mama, and then, "The *kinara* holds the light of tomorrow. Tomorrow holds the light of the *kinara*."

Chaka uses both hands to give Mama the *kinara*. Mama puts it in the middle of the table. From the box, Mama takes three green candles. Baba takes three red candles and puts them in the *kinara*, which is a candle holder, saying, "*Mshumaa* one, *mishumaa* two, *mishumaa* three." Mama puts her candles on the other side of the *kinara*, saying, "*Mishumaa* four, *mishumaa* five, *mishumaa* six."

Together they place a long black candle in the center. "*Mishumaa saba*, black as night, stands in the center of our *kinara's* light. Red for blood not shed in vain. Black for the continent from which we sprang. Green for hope and knowledge growing. Seven candles. Seven nights. Let love stand. Light our lives."

"Those candles are so beautifully nice," I say, and count them. "*Moja, mbili, tatu, nne, tano, sita, saba*." That's how you count to seven in Swahili, and Chaka does the exact same thing because he's such a copycat.

Well, not always, because before I can say "jack rabbit!" Chaka asks, "Can I light the candles, Mama? Can I, huh?"

"Chaka, we're going to light our *kinara* on the first day of Kwanzaa, which is the day after Christmas," Mama says. "Now, we just have a few more things to do. Let's put the *kikombe* cup on the table together."

Mama's hand, Baba's hand, Chaka's hand and mine put the *kikombe* cup close to the *kinara*. People are carved and crowded everywhere on the cup except inside. Our cup is from Africa. Baba says, "This cup is carved from the Tree of Life. You can't really see the tree because so many people are growing on it. The Tree of Life is an always-blooming tree and it's *always* crowded. When we drink from the *kikombe* cup it will be as if we're drinking a magical liquid gathered from a tree whose fruit sweetens the life of everyone, even generations to come."

"Baba, are we pretending we're drinking people from a cup?"

"Well, that's one way to think of it. Just remember that when we share the *kikombe* cup we'll be honoring those great people who gave of their lives to make life better for us. People like Harriet Tubman, Sojourner Truth, Martin Luther King, Jr., Malcolm X, W.E.B. DuBois, Marcus Garvey and many others whose names we'll never know."

"Kia, I've prepared something in the kitchen that you will know about," says Mama.

We follow her into the kitchen. She hands Baba a basket full of fruit.

"Coconut, banana, pineapple, apple. *Matunda ya kwanzaa* — our first fruit. Even though the fruit is from the supermarket, our basket of fruit is our little harvest. Just like a garden, each one of us is growing and will continue to grow, in many wonderful ways, for the rest of our lives. And here's a basket of vegetables. *Mboga ya kwanzaa* — our first vegetables."

"Ahhh, but these are extra special vegetables," says Baba. "Step right up so I can present you with our *vibunzi*, children. I have two ears of corn. One is for you, Chaka, and one for you, Kia. You've blessed *us* by being born into our family. Welcome, again and again!"

We make our own parade, marching from the kitchen to the living room with our baskets and corn. One by one, we put them on our Kwanzaa table.

"We sure know the meaning of *Ujima*," Mama says when we finish.

"What Jima, Mama, what Jima?" goes Chaka.

"That's when we work together. Just like everybody in our family working together to prepare for our Kwanzaa celebration."

"And now, good night sleepyheads! See you when the sun gets out of bed." Baba starts singing our good-night song. Then Chaka starts singing and I do too, all the way up the stairs.

9

Disemba 25 • December 25

In the morning, it's Christmas Day.

"Mama, is Grandmom having Kwanzaa?"

"Probably not," she says.

"Then what's she gonna do?"

"Have Christmas like always, and we'll spend Christmas with her, like always. In fact, I think she can use some help getting ready, don't you?"

I put on my red dress with the green velvet bows, wrap my presents and go to Grandmom's house.

"Grandmom, we're having Kwanzaa at our house!" I say when I get there.

"That so, babygirl. Tell me all about it while we finish decorating our tree."

By the time Baba, Mama and Chaka rang the doorbell, Grandmom knew all about Kwanzaa. I even made three Kwanzaa cards for her. On the first card I drew a picture of our Kwanzaa table. On the second, I drew a picture of the quilt on Grandmom's bed, and last I drew a picture of Great-Grandpop's old fiddle and tambourine because they're our history.

"Kia, your cards show lots of *Kuumba*," Baba says.

"That's another Kwanzaa word, isn't it, Baba?"

"Yep, and it celebrates your creativity."

"I got *Kuumba*, Kia," says Chaka.

"But not as much as me, Chaka. Creativity and Kia go together 'cause I'm a better drawer than you!"

Chaka starts whining and then crying. He's such a baby.

"*Harambee!* Let's pull together! Can we have some *Umoja* between you two today?" says Baba. "That means you, Kia, and you, Chaka, need to work on getting along together so we can have a pleasant Christmas dinner. Both of you are special in your own way. I have faith, *Imani*, that you know how to play quietly until we are ready for supper."

So Chaka and I start singing, "Creativity and Kia go together. Creativity and Chaka go together. And the forks, spoons and knives do, too!"

Disemba 26 December 26

Habari gani? What's the news?

Umoja! Unity!

Today is the first day of Kwanzaa! Mama is on vacation, but Baba has to work. Instead of saying "good morning," Mama says, *"Habari gani? What's the news?"*

Chaka says, "I hungry, Ma. I hungry."

But I say, *"Umoja!* You're supposed to say *Umoja*, Chaka!"

"I no want *Umoja*, Mama. I want cereal."

Chaka be so silly in the morning sometimes.

When Baba gets home, he says, *"Habari gani? What's the news?"*

Chaka and I say, *"Umoja,* Baba, *Umoja!* Let's have Kwanzaa!"

Everyone goes to the Kwanzaa table. Mama fills the *kikombe* cup with juice. Baba, Chaka and I light the big black candle. Each one of us drinks from the cup.

Then we say:

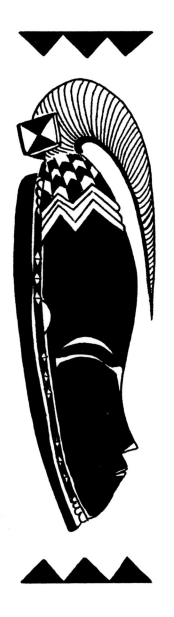

For our people everywhere
all over the world
for Africa our ancestral land
for our heroes and heroines
our children and our children's children
for our wise old
for our history our humanity
and our hearts holding love
a love that builds and binds
a love that gives and strengthens
united we remember
united we honor our lives
the lives of our ancestors
of our generations to come
together we stand
together we join hands
Harambee! Harambee! Harambee!
Harambee! Harambee! Harambee!
Harambee!

Disemba 27 December 27

Habari gani? What's the news?

Kujichagulia! Self-determination!

Mama says that today Chaka and I can do anything we want to do. We just have to plan how we want to spend our day.

Chaka says, " I want to play with Markie."

"Is that all you want to do all day, Chaka? Can you think of one more thing?"

"Can Markie and me go to the park and fly, Mama?"

"You mean fly your new kite? We can go for a little while if it isn't too cold."

"I want to go to the library with Martina, Mama." Martina is my best friend. "And then I want to come home and fix sandwiches for Martina and me so we can have a picnic right on the living room rug with a tablecloth and everything!"

At dinner, I tell Baba how Chaka and I got to plan our whole day.

"That's what self-determination means, Kia. It means you get to decide how you want to do something. The decisions we make in our lives are very important."

Each night the *kinara's* light gets brighter. Tonight, we light the black candle and a red one. Baba pours the juice and we drink from our *kikombe* cup and say our *Harambee*s just like before.

Disemba 28 | December 28

Habari gani? What's the news?

Ujima! Collective work and responsibility!

Today is Mama's day to plan something for us to do. "Look in your closet for clothes that are too small for you," she says.

Chaka and I have big paper bags for our clothes. I put a doll I don't want anymore into mine. When I finish I help Chaka.

Mama drives us to a shelter where a friend of hers works. While Mama talks with Mrs. Collins, Chaka and I get to play with our toys for one last time. I meet a girl named Taray.

"I have lots of friends," says Taray. "When I go home I'm gonna play with all of them again, especially Diona, BeeBee and Latrice. And I'm never gonna come back here 'cause I miss where I used to live and never get to visit. Why you giving your pretty baby away? What's her name?"

"Her name's Sukie. See, I braided her braids and made these dresses."

"My mama says we're gonna be out of here soon. She says we're gonna find a better place to live. Do you wanna see my dolls?"

"What are their names?" I ask when she shows me.

"This is Bunny and this one's name is KayKay. They were feeling really sad, but now we have a new friend. Ask your mama if you can come and play with us."

Tonight, we light a red, a black, and a green candle.

"Bright, bright *kinara* light," I say before we drink from our *kikombe* cup.

"Let's make a wish for all the families living in shelters," Mama says, and we do. I wish my wish last. I hope it comes forever ever true.

Disemba 29 | December 29

Habari gani? What's the news?

Ujamaa! Cooperative economics!

Mama has a doctor's appointment today. While she's gone I'm going to help out at Another Village. Another Village is a bookstore. They have lots of books and a special section for kids. Miss Martha owns it. The store's really crowded because it's the week after Christmas and lots of books are on sale. I get to help right away!

"Kia, would you like to recommend a book to this lady for her grand-child?" Miss Martha asks.

I show the lady two of my favorite books and she buys them.

I help Miss Martha in many different ways. I hand out receipts, put books in bags, and show kids to the children's section if they are new to the store. After things slow down, Miss Martha shows me how to ring up a sale. Then, she pays me!

"You're a great salesgirl, Kia Edwards. I enjoy working with you. You're welcome to come back and help out anytime," she says.

I can't wait to come back and help Miss Martha. I already know what I'm going to do with my money. First, I'll save it, and then, when I have enough money, I *know* which book I'm going to buy!

Disemba 30   December 30

Habari gani? What's the news?

Nia! Purpose!

Today, Baba is home. On weekends, he and his friends, Mr. Carrington, Mr. Davis, Mr. Winfield, Brother Davenport and my uncle Chuck, have a sort of club. They go around and help people fix things. They help elderly people, people from our community center and each other. Today, Baba and Brother Davenport are shoveling Sister Ruth's walk. While they're shoveling, Sister Ruth and I make hot apple cider and zucchini bread. I even have a loaf to take home.

When they come in it's brrr so cold! "When can we go home, Baba? I wanna show Mama my zucchini bread."

"When we're finished shoveling, Kia. We're just taking a break, so please be patient. Being a good neighbor means we can't leave until the job is done. Being involved in our community is what *Nia* is all about. I was taught how to be a good neighbor when I was a kid in South Carolina. Just because we're in Philadelphia is no reason to stop. So, scratch my back and I'll scratch yours!"

I scratch him hard-hard.

"Kia, you're such a good back scratcher!"

I can feel his voice tingling through my fingers and hand. Then Baba scratches my back. Baba doesn't really scratch. He tickles!

Disemba 31 December 31

Habari gani? What's the news?

Kuumba! Creativity!

Hooray! We're going to the Afro-American Museum for a special Kwanzaa program today.

When we arrive we see an exhibit about African people from all over the world. "There are people of African descent in the Caribbean, Central and South America and every little nook and cranny in the world," Mama says. "There are some of us everywhere."

But, best of best, my friends Aisha and Zahida are here! Aisha belongs to the Mujaji Dance Theatre. Zahida and I sit together, right up front, and watch. Aisha dances to a southern African rain goddess. She pretends that she wants Mujaji the Rain Goddess to rain on her crops. Aisha becomes a rain cloud, a rainbow and even the thunder and lightning!

Afterwards, we make beaded "love letters" to send to kids in South Africa. Each color has a special meaning. The museum lady says I might even get a real letter back if I put my address on my card. I draw a tiny picture of myself and write, "I will be happy when South Africa is free. Then, maybe, you can come visit me. Love, Kia."

Habari gani? What's the news?

Imani! Faith!

Tonight is the last night of Kwanzaa. We are having a *karamu*, a feast. We have African, Caribbean and African-American food for our feast. Things like ginger beer, peanut soup, yams, collard greens, barbecue chicken, gumbo, jambalaya and callaloo. Martina, Aisha and Zahida are here. And guess who? Taray! Miss Martha and Sister Ruth have come. Markie and Grandmom, too. My Baba's buddies and their families are coming one by one.

"Mama, can we light the candles now?"

"Yes, and make sure everyone gets a turn."

With a long match Martina lights a candle. She passes it to Aisha. Zahida, Markie, Chaka and Taray light a candle. I light the black one last. The *kinara* shines brighty-bright.

Baba pours a libation just like they do in Africa. He takes a sip from the *kikombe* cup and then he passes it around.

"We have much to share tonight," he says, "about Africa, the Caribbean, the Americas and these United States. While we remember our past, let's prepare economically, educationally, politically and spiritually for our future.

"For those of us blessed with children — enjoy, encourage, love and help them in every way you can. They are our future. We are their history. *Habari gani?*"

"*Imani!*" we answer.

"I have faith," Baba continues, "that we will continue to grow as a people and that each one of us will find a light that shines as bright as the *kinara's* light tonight. I have faith that we will teach and learn from each other at the same time. Let our learning begin. Happy New Year!"

We exchange our *zawadi*, our gifts. Books and bookmarks with names of people who are important to our history and our lives are the kinds of *zawadi* we exchange.

We make a giant circle. Everyone gets quiet, the kind of quiet where you can hear people breathing and, maybe, their hearts beating, too. But we're not quiet for long. Just like a chorus we say, again and again,

"Hey, hey, Harambee!

Let's pull together today!

Here's my hand.

In love we stand.

Together!"

NGUZO SABA • The Seven Principles

UMOJA (oo-MOH-jah) • *Unity*
To strive for and to maintain unity in the family, community, nation and race.

KUJICHAGULIA (koo-GEE-cha-GOO-lee-ah) • *Self-determination*
To define ourselves, name ourselves, create for ourselves and speak for ourselves instead of being defined, created for and spoken for by others.

UJIMA (oo-GEE-mah) • *Collective Work and Responsibility*
To build and maintain our community together, and to make our sisters' and brothers' problems our problems and to solve them together.

UJAMAA (oo-JAH-mah) • *Cooperative Economics*
To build and maintain our own stores, shops and other businesses and to profit from them together.

NIA (NEE-ah) • *Purpose*
To make our collective vocation the building and developing of our community in order to restore our people to their traditional greatness.

KUUMBA (koo-OOM-bah) • *Creativity*
To do always as much as we can, in the way we can, in order to leave our community more beautiful and beneficial than we inherited it.

IMANI (ee-MAH-nee) • *Faith*
To believe with all our heart in our people, our parents, our teachers, our leaders and the righteousness and victory of our struggle.

Maulana Karenga, 7 September 1965

31

GLOSSARY

Beaded love letters • beaded medallions, usually rectangular, made by the Xhosa, Zulu and Ndebele peoples of South Africa. Color represents the message: red – "my love is true"; blue – "go in peace". . .

Bendera ya taifa (ben-DER-ah yah tah-ee-fah) • a flag or standard whose colors, black, red and green, are symbolic of African-American struggle and heritage.

Callaloo (CAL-lah-loo) • a popular, leafy vegetable similar to kale or spinach, indigenous to the Caribbean. A soup which is a staple on almost every Caribbean island.

Ginger beer • a homemade soft drink brewed from fresh ginger popular in sub-Saharan Africa and the Caribbean.

Gumbo (GUM-boh) • originated from the Bantu language and, in that language, means okra. A stew consisting of okra, vegetables, meat and/or seafood with French, Spanish and African influences, originating in Louisiana.

Habari gani (hah-BAR-ree GAH-nee) • Swahili for "What's new?" and adapted for the purposes of Kwanzaa by M. Karenga to "What news?"

Harambee (hah-RAHM-bay) • a chant continental Africans used when engaged in pulling a heavy object. It literally means "Let's pull together."

Jambalaya (JAHM-bah-li-YAH) • a rice dish cooked with ham, sausage, chicken, shrimp or oysters and seasoned with herbs.

Karamu (kah-RAH-moo) • a feast in which food is contributed by each participating family or person. Before and during the Karamu an informative and entertaining program is presented.

Kente cloth (KEN-tay) • woven strips of bright silk, 8' to 10' long, sewn together into cloth. Once worn only by Ghanian kings and high-ranking chiefs, it is now worn by many Ghanians on formal occasions. Contemporary copies and original kente cloth are used for gift wrap, clothing and accessories.

Kikombe cup (kee-KOOM-bay) • the unity cup that is used to pour libations to ancestors and then shared in honor of the struggles and achievements of African-Americans.

Kinara (kee-NAH-rah) • a candle holder which represents continental Africa and Kwanzaa's stress on African origins and African-American identity.

Libation (li-BAY-shun) • ceremonious pouring and/or drinking of an alcoholic or non-alcoholic drink

Matunda ya kwanza (mah-TOON-dah yah KWAHN-zah) • "first fruits," the Kiswahili phrase from which Kwanzaa was derived.

Mazao (mah-ZAH-oo) • based on the agricultural ceremonies of African peoples, Kwanzaa is a harvest festival, in its broadest sense. That is, it is a time for celebration, rejoicing, togetherness, thanksgiving and reinforcement of communal bonds. The mazao are crops, the bounty that results from productive labor and common effort.

Mbili (mm-BEE-lee) • two.

Mishumaa saba (mee-SHOO-mah SAH-bah) • representative of the seven principles on which Kwanzaa is based. A candle is lit daily in honor of each principle. Singular — mshumaa; plural — mishumaa.

Mkeka (mm-KAY-kah) • a mat that symbolizes tradition and, by extension, history, given its use in traditional African society.

Moja (MOH-jah) • one.

Nne (nn-NAY) • four.

Saba (SAH-bah) • seven.

Sita (SEE-tah) • six.

Swahili (swa-HEE-lee) • a Bantu language that is spoken over much of East Africa, particularly in Burundi, Kenya, Tanzania, Zaire, Zambia and the Congo and Somali Republics.

Tambiko (tam-BEE-ko) • a libation poured to African and African-American ancestors from the *kikombe* cup while making a *tamshi la tambiko*, a libation statement.

Tano (TAH-noh) • five.

Tatu (TAH-too) • three.

Vibunzi (vee-BOON-zee) • corn. Each ear of corn symbolizes each child in a family. Kwanzaa places emphasis on children, as they bring new potential and prosperity to their families.

Zawadi (zah-WAH-dee) • a gift consisting of a book and an African or African-American heritage symbol.